Murgatroyd's Garden

Judy Zavos · Drahos Zak

SIMON & SCHUSTER

william

A WATERMARK PRESS BOOK

MURGATROYD'S GARDEN was created and produced by
The Watermark Press
Sydney, Australia

First published in Great Britain by
Simon & Schuster Limited 1987

© 1986 The Watermark Press
© Text Judy Zavos
© Illustrations Drahos Zak
Reprinted (three times) 1987

Simon & Schuster Limited, West Garden Place,
Kendal Street, London W2 2AQ

British Library Cataloguing in Publication Data

Zavos, Judy
Murgatroyd's garden.
I. Title II. Zak, Drahos
823[J] PZ7

ISBN 0-671-65305-9

Printed in Hong Kong

Once upon a time, there was a little boy called Murgatroyd.

Murgatroyd lived with his Mummy and Daddy in a
nice house in a big city.

He was a very happy boy. He had lots of lovely things to
play with, and his Mummy and Daddy loved him very much.

There was only one problem. He hated, hated, hated having his hair washed. Every time his Mummy or Daddy said, "Come along Murgatroyd, it's time we washed your hair", he would start to scream.

Now Murgatroyd's screams were not like any screams you've ever heard.

They were AMAZING.

They were so piercing that they sounded like
a million little boys screaming.
They were so fierce that they sounded like
a million lions roaring.
And they were so loud that people could hear
them EVERYWHERE.

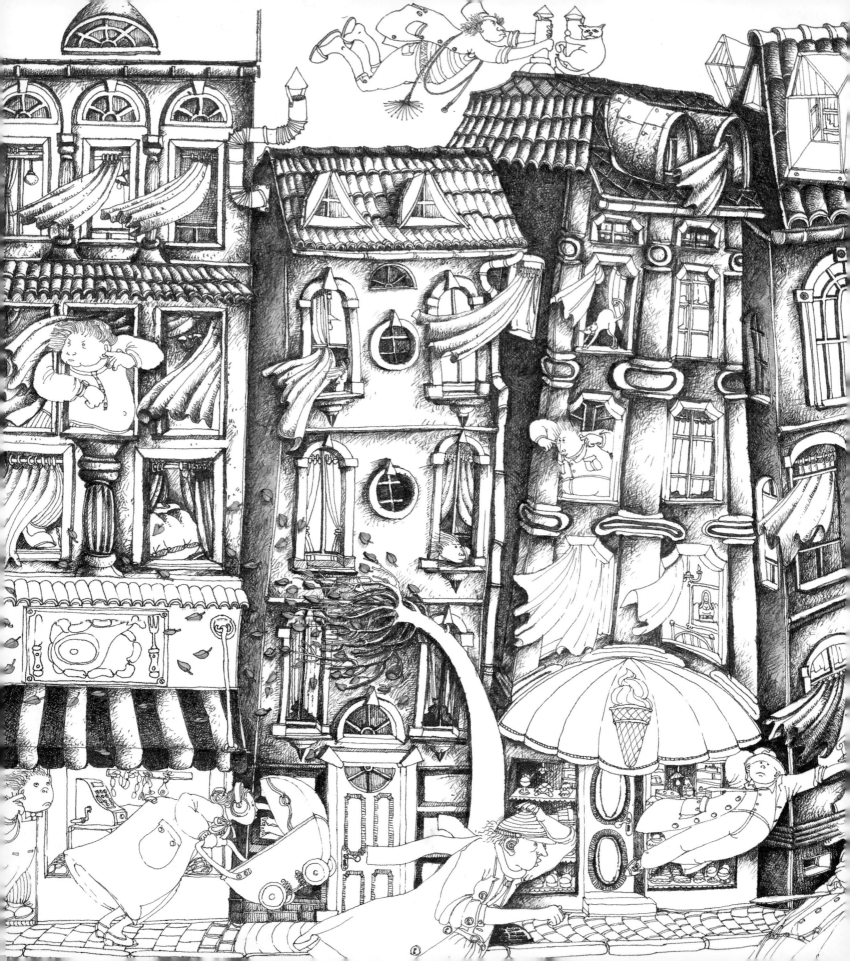

Everyone was getting headaches.
They were buying ear-muffs to keep
out the sound.

They could hear Murgatroyd's screams
across the road and down the street
and even in the next neighbourhood.

They could hear them in the next city,
which was a long, long way away.

The Mayor was giving an important speech in the Council Chamber when the screams grew so loud that nobody in the audience could hear what he was saying.

The Queen heard them as she was getting
ready for a very important occasion. She was
so surprised, she dropped her crown and
broke it.

The President was just getting ready to board the
Presidential jet when he heard the screams. He thought
it was the noise of the plane taking off and in his
hurry to get on board, he dropped all his important
papers.

Murgatroyd's Mummy and Daddy started getting very worried. The Mayor, the Queen and the President were sending them urgent messages demanding that they stop the screaming.

But what could they do?

They begged and begged Murgatroyd to let them wash his hair without screaming.

They offered to make special Murgatroyd Hairwash Goggles for him.
They offered to make special Murgatroyd Shampoo for him.
They promised him that they would be very gentle.

But Murgatroyd continued to scream. One day it got so bad that the Mayor called a special meeting with the Queen and the President and all their special advisors.

"What shall we do?" they asked each other.

They talked and thought, thought and talked, all through the night. Finally, the Mayor had a bright idea. "If Murgatroyd hates having his hair washed so much," he said, "then let us ask his parents to stop washing his hair."

So an urgent telegram arrived at Murgatroyd's house.
"No more hair washes, by order of the Mayor"
it read.

Murgatroyd's Mummy and Daddy were very upset.
"Murgatroyd's hair will be filthy", they said.

Murgatroyd just smiled.

One week went by, then two, three, four, five, six, seven, eight, nine, ten. Nobody could believe how peaceful it was without those screams.

Babies were sleeping right through the night. Cats and dogs snoozed from bedtime till breakfast time. People threw away their aspirins and their ear-muffs.

In the tenth week of peace and quiet, something very strange happened. Murgatroyd started to grow a garden on his head!

Do you know why? His hair had become so dirty that
things started to grow in it!

At first, nobody worried very much about it. Murgatroyd's Mummy just picked the flowers and put them in vases. Soon the house was overflowing with flowers.

Then there were so many flowers that the neighbours started to pick them too. People came from all over the city to pick the lovely flowers from Murgatroyd's garden.

Soon, Murgatroyd became very famous again. People from all over the country heard about the amazing garden which was growing on a little boy's head.

Garden experts said, "What rubbish! Gardens grow in gardens, not on heads!" Nobody could believe it. People came from all over the world to see for themselves.

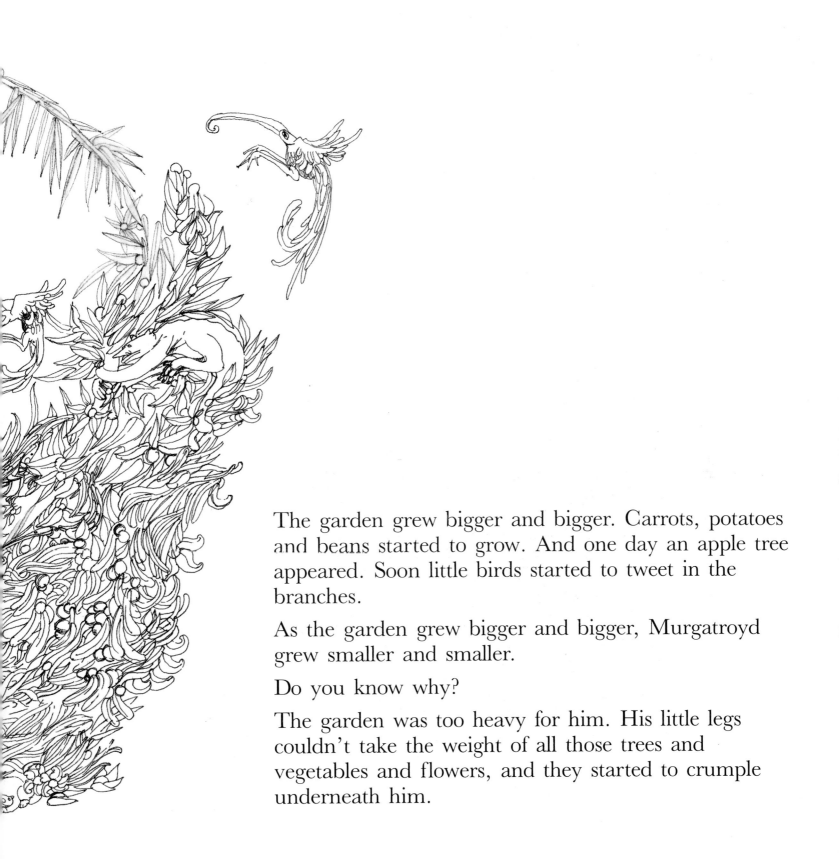

The garden grew bigger and bigger. Carrots, potatoes and beans started to grow. And one day an apple tree appeared. Soon little birds started to tweet in the branches.

As the garden grew bigger and bigger, Murgatroyd grew smaller and smaller.

Do you know why?

The garden was too heavy for him. His little legs couldn't take the weight of all those trees and vegetables and flowers, and they started to crumple underneath him.

Murgatroyd just sat there day after day getting more and more miserable, while the flowers grew prettier and prettier, the carrots and apples got bigger and juicier, all kinds of animals made themselves at home in the undergrowth, and the birds twittered happily in the trees.

Even Murgatroyd got worried now. His Mummy and Daddy were terribly worried — soon there would be all garden and no Murgatroyd. They rang up the Mayor and the Queen and the President and told them what had happened.

Everyone agreed that the garden had to go.

So Murgatroyd's Mummy and Daddy got busy shooing away the birds and animals, chopping down the juicy apple trees, digging up the yummy carrots, potatoes and beans, and pulling out all the lovely flowers. Then they went out to buy ear-muffs and aspirins.

Then what do you think they did?

They WASHED MURGATROYD'S HAIR, of course!

And something very surprising happened. Murgatroyd was so pleased to be able to stand up straight again, that he actually thanked his Mummy and Daddy for washing his hair.

"Thank you, thank you Mummy and Daddy, I like my hair clean. I promise I'll never scream again", he said.

And he didn't. And now Murgatroyd is as tall and straight
as you. He still lives happily with his Mummy and
Daddy in a nice house in a city not far from here.
And his hair is lovely and clean.